SITWE JOSEPH
GOES TO WORSHIP

Story by
Twesigye Jackson Kaguri

Art by
Dennis Caleb Kiirya

1

Sitwe Joseph Goes to Worship by Twesigye Jackson Kaguri

Art by Dennis Caleb Kiirya

Copyright: Twesigye Jackson Kaguri

Special thanks to Susan Urbanek Linville

Published by Nyaka AIDS Orphans Project, PO Box 339, East Lansing, MI 48826

May 2015

ISBN-13: 978-1512019438

ISBN-10: 1512019437

Sitwe Joseph Books

Sitwe Joseph Goes to School
Sitwe Joseph Goes to Worship

Sitwe was studying his arithmetic when Mukaaka peered into their hut.

"Where is Stephen?" she said.

"Sleeping," Sitwe said. He waved across the room. The last time he saw Stephen, he was sleeping under the mosquito net.

"He is not there," Mukaaka said.

Sitwe put down his papers. "I do not understand, How could he escape?"

Mukaaka shook her head. "When you read books you go to another world. Run to Mr. Twine's plantation. Stephen is probably visiting the chickens again."

"Do I have to?" Sitwe was tired after his long walk from school. "I must study for my test."

"Go now," Mukaaka said. "It will be night soon."

Sitwe trudged down the grassy road leading to Mr. Twine's house. Tall thorny hedges blocked the fields to his right. Banana trees stretched down the hill to his left.

Sitwe practiced his multiplication. "Two times one is two. Two times two is four. Two times three is six."

He wished his older sister, Komo, was not staying late at Nyaka School. It would be her job to chase Stephen.

"Two times four is eight. Two times five is ten."

"Help!" a voice yelled from beyond the hedge.
"Heelp!

"Stephen!" Sitwe said. "Is that you?"

Sitwe went to his knees and peered under the thorny hedge. All he could see was tall grass and a small grove of trees. An ente mooed in the distance.

A crow coasted across the path and landed in a tree.

"Trouble. Trouble," it cawed.

"Stephen!" Sitwe yelled. "Stephen!"

"Sitwe?" Stephen sobbed. "Where are you?"

Sitwe looked for a way through the hedge, but it was too thorny. "Hold on," he said. "I am on my way."

Sitwe rushed up the path. He searched for a gap wide enough to squeeze through.

Stephen cried harder.

"Don't worry," Sitwe said. "I'm almost there."

Sitwe found an opening and crawled through. Thorns grabbed his shirt and cut his arms.

"Ouch."

He stood, but could not see Stephen

"Where are you?" he yelled.

The crow flew to the grove. "Here. Here," it cawed.

Sitwe dashed through the grass to the trees.

The trunks had been cut for fire wood many times. The bottoms that were left were jagged and sharp. New trees grew from old roots.

"Mukaaka told us not to play in here," Sitwe said. He climbed over uneven stumps.

"Sitwe. Sitwe." Stephen sobbed.

"I'm coming," Sitwe said.

Sitwe found Stephen lying on his back. A large piece of wood had stabbed through his leg. And there was blood.

"Help me," Stephen cried. "My leg hurts."

Sitwe felt sick to his stomach. He didn't want to look, but he had to be brave.

"Everything will be okay," he said. Inside he was panicking. This was bad, really bad. Stephen had been in trouble before, but not like this.

"I'm going to lift you," Sitwe said. He reached down and pulled his brother by the arms.

Stephen screamed. His leg pulled free of the wood. Blood gushed from the wound.

Oh, no, Sitwe thought. *We need a doctor.* The nearest hospital was far away in Kambuga.

"Help. Help," the crow cawed.

Sitwe wrapped his shirt around Stephen's leg. The bleeding slowed, but did not stop.

"I want Mukaaka," Stephen cried.

"So do I," Sitwe said. He lifted Stephen in his arms and struggled over the old stumps.

What could Mukaaka do? Stephen needed to go to the hospital. They needed a truck. Maybe Mr. Twine could help them.

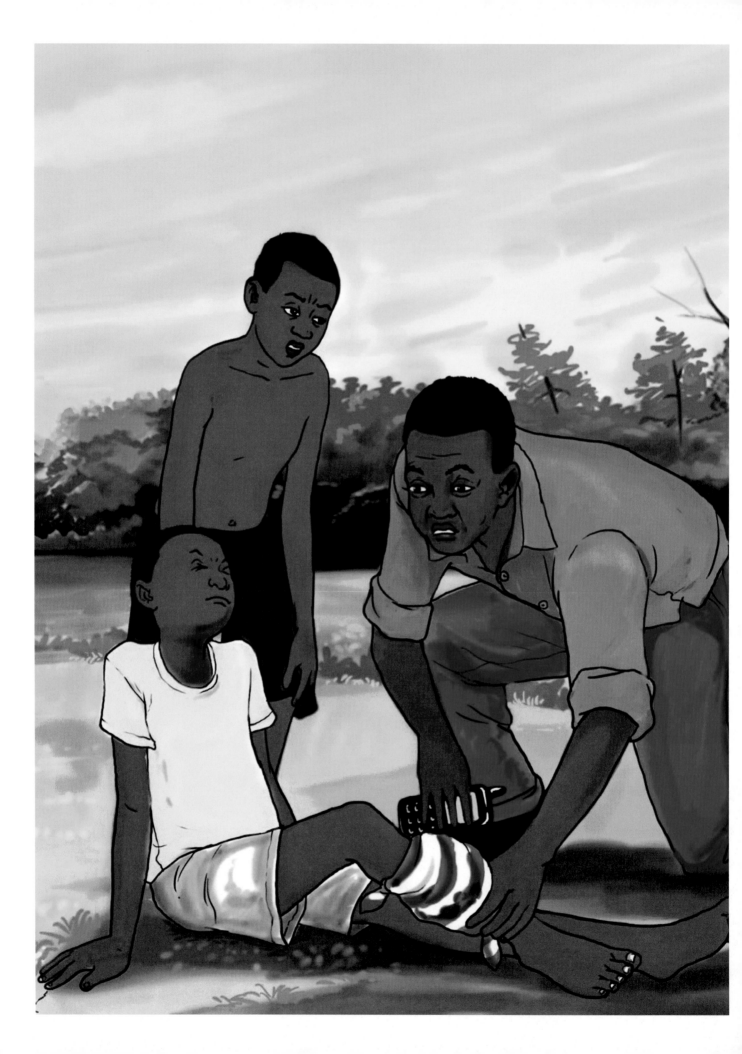

Sitwe carried Stephen across the field. They had to go around the thorny fence, which seemed to take forever. He walked as fast as he could to Mr. Twine's large brick house.

Three goats stood staked in the front yard. Chickens wandered through the tall grass.

"Mr. Twine!" Sitwe called. "Stephen is bleeding."

Mr. Twine came quickly. He looked at the wound with a frown. Stephen's eyes were closed and his skin pale.

"He fell," Sitwe said. "He was climbing in the trees."

Mr. Twine kneeled next to Stephen. "He needs to go to the hospital."

Mr. Twine called someone with his cell phone.

"My brother is bringing his truck," he said.

It took a long time for the truck to arrive. It was full of green bananas in the back.

Mr. Twine lifted Sitwe into the cab and then followed. He held Stephen on his lap.

"This is a very bad wound," he said to the driver. "Please drive as fast as is safe."

"I was supposed to be watching him," Sitwe said. "He was climbing a tree. It is my fault."

"Do not blame yourself," Mr. Twine said. "Accidents happen."

They bounced from the grassy road onto a larger road that was gravel and dirt. Houses here were built of brick instead of thatch and mud. It took him an hour every morning to travel this road to school. In the truck, it took a few minutes, but those minutes seemed too long.

By the time they reached the hospital, Stephen was limp in Mr. Twine's arms.

Sitwe wanted to ask Mr. Twine if his brother was going to die, but he was afraid. If he said the words, it might come true.

A nurse in a white dress was busy with several patients. At first she ignored them. When she finally looked up, her eyes grew wide. Without saying a word, she took Stephen from Mr. Twine's arms and rushed him down the hall.

"You wait here," Mr. Twine said. "I will get your mukaaka and bring her to hospital."

Sitwe sat next to an old man. He felt alone and afraid.

"Two times two is four." He should have been watching his brother, not studying mathematics.

"Sitwe Joseph?"

Sitwe looked up. It was Pastor Saul from Nyaka School. He taught Bible class each week. Sitwe's favorite stories were about the animals on Noah's Ark, and Jesus making bread and fish for people.

"What are you doing here?" Pastor Saul asked.

"My brother hurt his leg," Sitwe said. "There was lots of blood."

"I am afraid Stephen will die," Sitwe said.

Pastor Saul sat beside him and opened his Bible. "Do you want to pray?" he said.

"I don't know how," Sitwe said.

Pastor Saul nodded.

"This is the book of Matthew ," he said. "In Chapter 8 it tells how God's son, Jesus, healed many people."

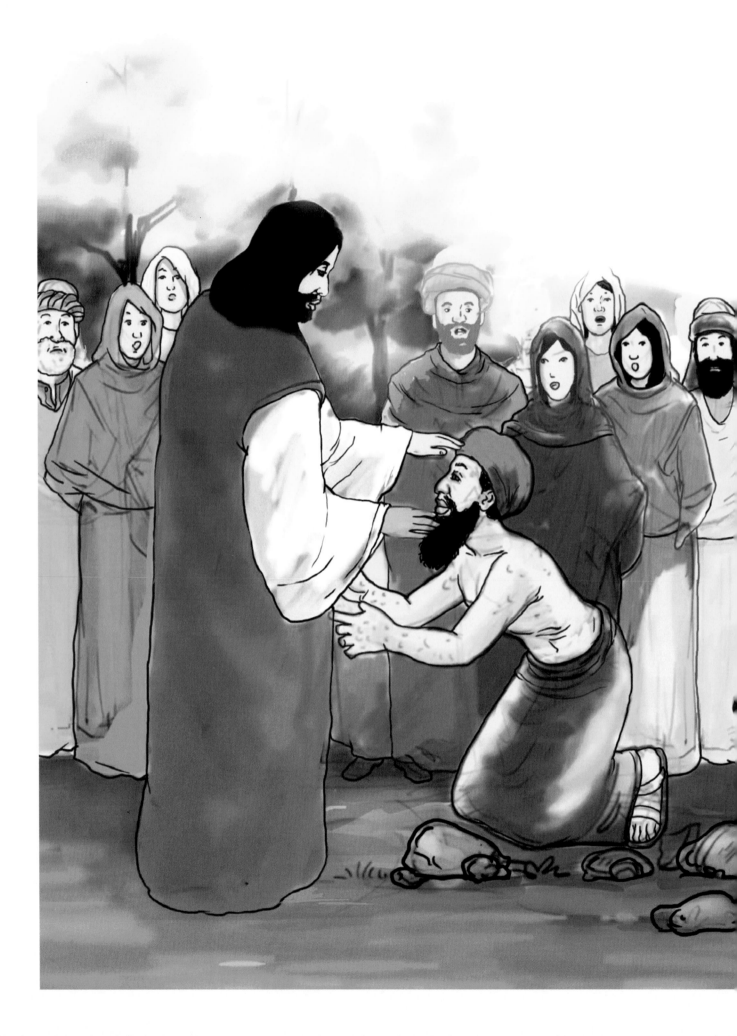

"Here it says that Jesus came down from the mountain. Many, many people followed him," Pastor Saul said.

"A man with a disease called leprosy came to him. He asked Jesus to make him clean. Jesus put forth his hand and touched him. He said: thou be clean. And immediately his leprosy was gone."

"Next, Jesus went into a town called Capernaum," Pastor Saul said. "A centurion, that's a Roman soldier, came to him. The soldier told Jesus that his servant was at home suffering with palsy. And Jesus said to him, I will come and heal him."

"The soldier said, 'Lord I am not worthy that thou should come under my roof; but speak the word only, and my servant shall be healed.'"

Pastor Saul turned the page.

"Jesus was surprised that the soldier had such faith," Pastor Saul said. "He told the soldier to return home. When the solder arrived home, he found his servant healed."

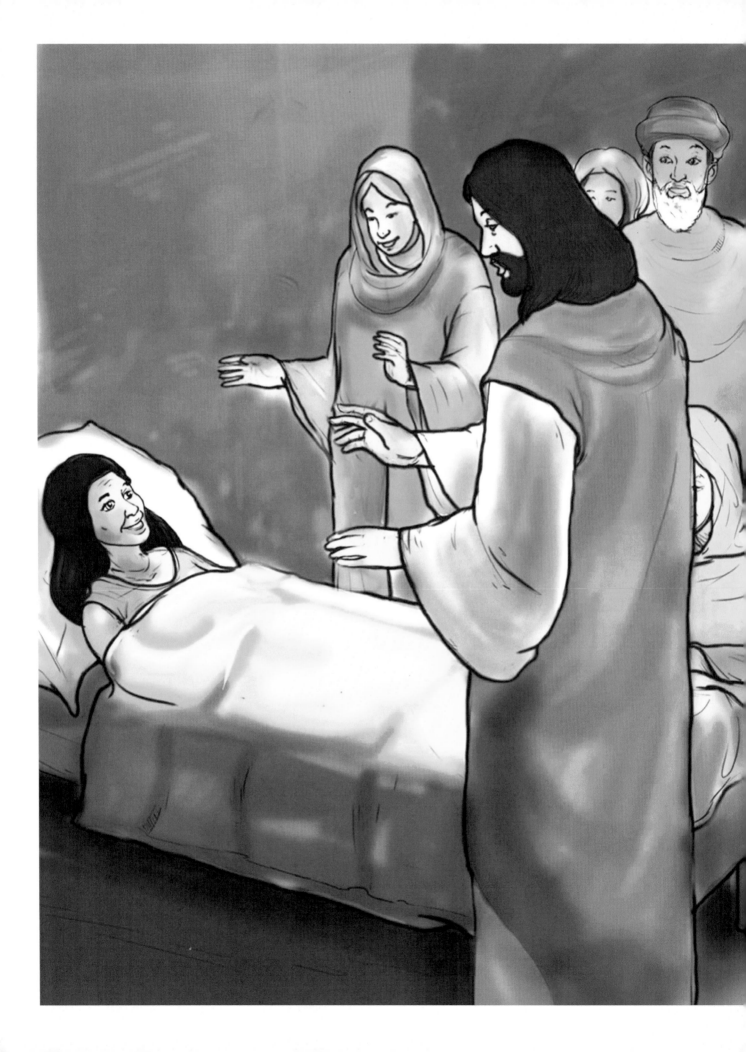

"Jesus went to Peter's house after that. He saw that Peter's mother-in-law was sick in bed with fever. He touched her hand, and the fever left her. She climbed from her bed and cared for them."

"Jesus isn't here," Sitwe said.

Pastor Saul smiled. "God is with us all the time," he said. "He is here in spirit. He is in your heart. "

"Can God help heal Stephen?" Sitwe said.

"If you pray, he will listen."

"He will?" Sitwe said.

"Yes, he will."

Mukaaka and Komo rushed through the hospital door. Mr. Twine followed.

"Where is my little boy?" Mukaaka said. "Where is my Stephen?"

The nurse behind the desk stood. "He is with the doctor," she said.

"I want to see him," she said. "Now!"

"You must wait," the nurse said. "He is in surgery."

They waited and waited.

Mr. Twine returned home.

Pastor Saul stood and patted Sitwe's head. "I must return to my church," he said. "If you need me, you can find me there."

They waited some more. Komo complained about being hungry. Mukaaka complained about the hard chairs.

Sitwe prayed in a whisper.

"Can you hear me in my heart, God? Please heal Stephen like Jesus did the leper."

A full moon was high in the sky when the doctor came to talk to them.

"I have taken out all the splinters and sewed up the wound," he said. "Now we must worry about infection."

"Can I see my boy?" Mukaaka said.

"Yes," the doctor said.

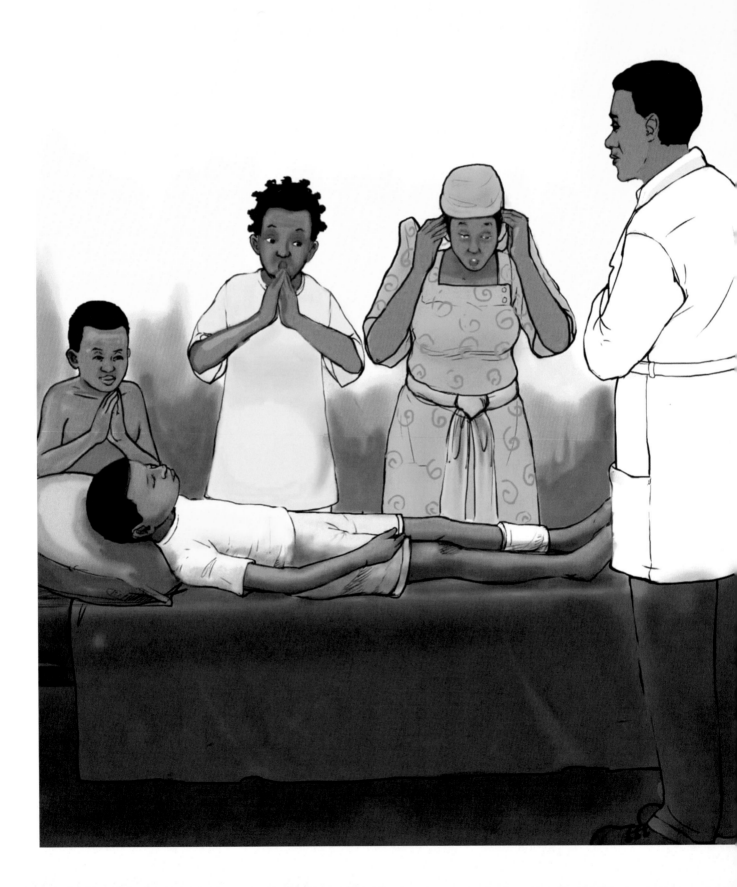

They walked through a ward with many patients. Stephen looked very small sleeping in such a big bed. His head was wet with fever.

Mukaaka took his hand. "Everything will be all right," she said. Still, she looked worried.

"Are you there, God?" Sitwe prayed. "Please heal Stephen. I promise to watch him all the time. This will never happen again."

"Find an extra blanket," Mukaaka said. "We will spend the night here."

The next morning Sitwe woke early. Mukaaka and Komo were asleep on the floor beside Stephen's bed.

Sitwe felt his brother's hand. It was very hot.

Maybe God had not heard his prayer. He had to do something. He would go to Pastor Saul.

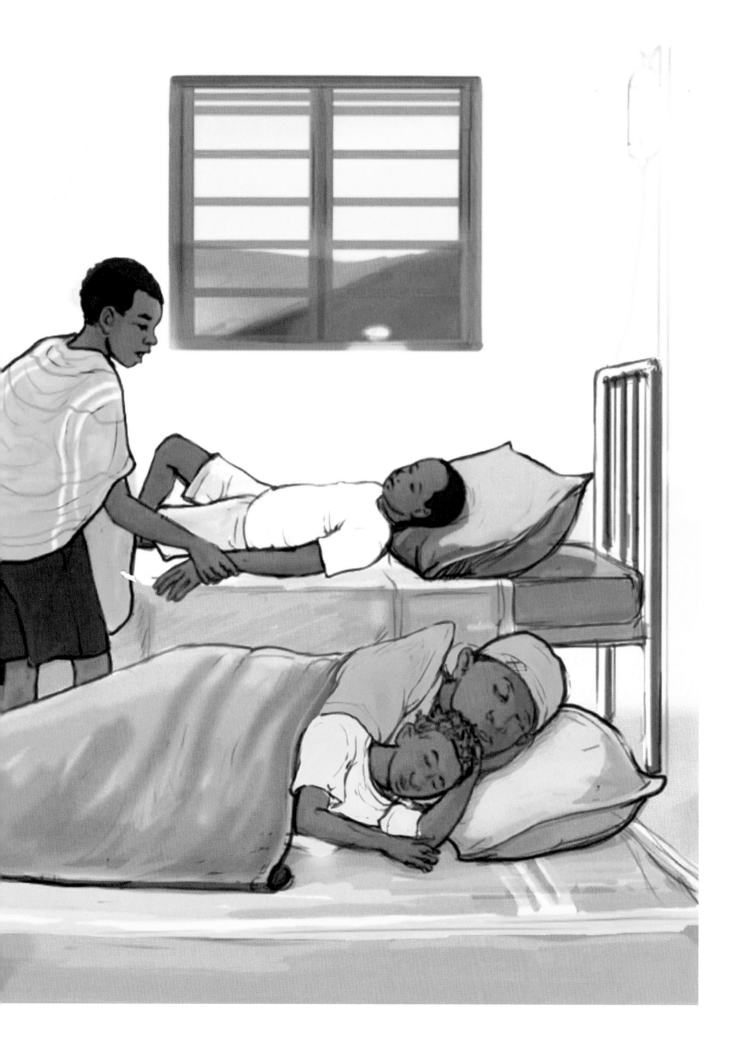

Sitwe ran to the church.

When he arrived, he found it full of people. They sat on long benches. Pastor Saul stood at the front with a Bible in his hands.

When Pastor Saul looked up, he stopped. Sitwe felt embarrassed for interrupting him. He backed from the doorway.

"Stay," Pastor Saul said. "All are welcome in the Lord's house."

People turned and looked. Sitwe wasn't sure what to do.

"Please join us," Pastor Saul said. He told the people about Stephen's accident. "Let us pray."

They prayed. They sang. Pastor Saul read from a book called Psalms. The story was about walking in darkness without fear.

After the church service, Pastor Saul gave Sitwe a Bible of his very own. The Pastor and three men walked back to the hospital with Sitwe. They prayed and sang on the way.

When they arrived, they found Mukaaka and Komo standing near Stephen's bed, smiling.

"The fever is gone," Mukaaka said.

Sitwe had never felt so happy.

"Thank the Lord," Pastor Saul said.

Sitwe held his Bible tightly. Next week he would go back to Pastor Saul's church. He wanted to learn more about the stories in the Bible. He wanted to know more about prayer.

Most of all, he wanted to thank God for helping Stephen.

Sitwe lives in Uganda. Uganda is a small country in East Africa.

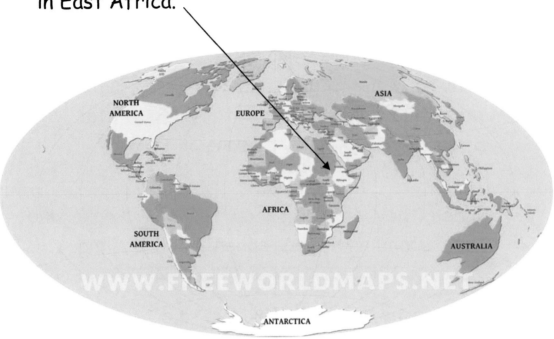

People in Uganda originally practiced traditional African religions. These included oral scriptures, the belief in a supreme creator, praying to spirits, respecting ancestors, the use of magic and traditional medicine.

In the 1860s, Muslim traders and Christian missionaries brought their religions to the Uganda.

Today there are large Mosques and Cathedrals as well as small rural houses of worship in Uganda.

Uganda is 85% Christian. The main Christian religions are: Roman Catholic, Anglican, Pentecostal, Seventh Day Adventist, and Orthodox Christian. Other religions include Muslim, (12%), Traditional (1%) , Judaism and Bahai.

HELP MAKE A DIFFERENCE

Visit www.nyakaschool.org for more information about the Nyaka AIDS Orphans Project.

Become a Friend of the Nyaka on Facebook, or become Jackson's friend there. You can also follow Jackson on Twitter at twitter.com/twejaka.

If you want to read more, check out the book, *A School for My Village,* on Amazon or at your local bookstore or library.

Form a Friends of Nyaka Group or join one in your area. Our friends Groups help spread the message. Check out our web site to learn how you can start a group in your community.

Become a Young Hero for Nyaka. Some Young Heroes have gathered books, collected relative's pocket change, and dedicated birthday money for donation.

For more information:

Nyaka AIDS Orphans Project
PO Box 339
East Lansing, MI 48826
info@nyakaschool.org
(517) 575-6623

Made in the USA
Lexington, KY
28 November 2017